CAPTAIN CUDDLES

MAUDIE POWELL-TUCK
JULIO ANTONIO BLASCO

LITTLE TIGER

LONDON

He can stop a rascally robbery . . .

Halt a runaway train . . .

And get this: he wears
a cape, a mask, and
a MASSIVE pair of . . .

PANTS!

HOLY MOLY!

Watch out, Captain Cuddles!

It's a **trap!**

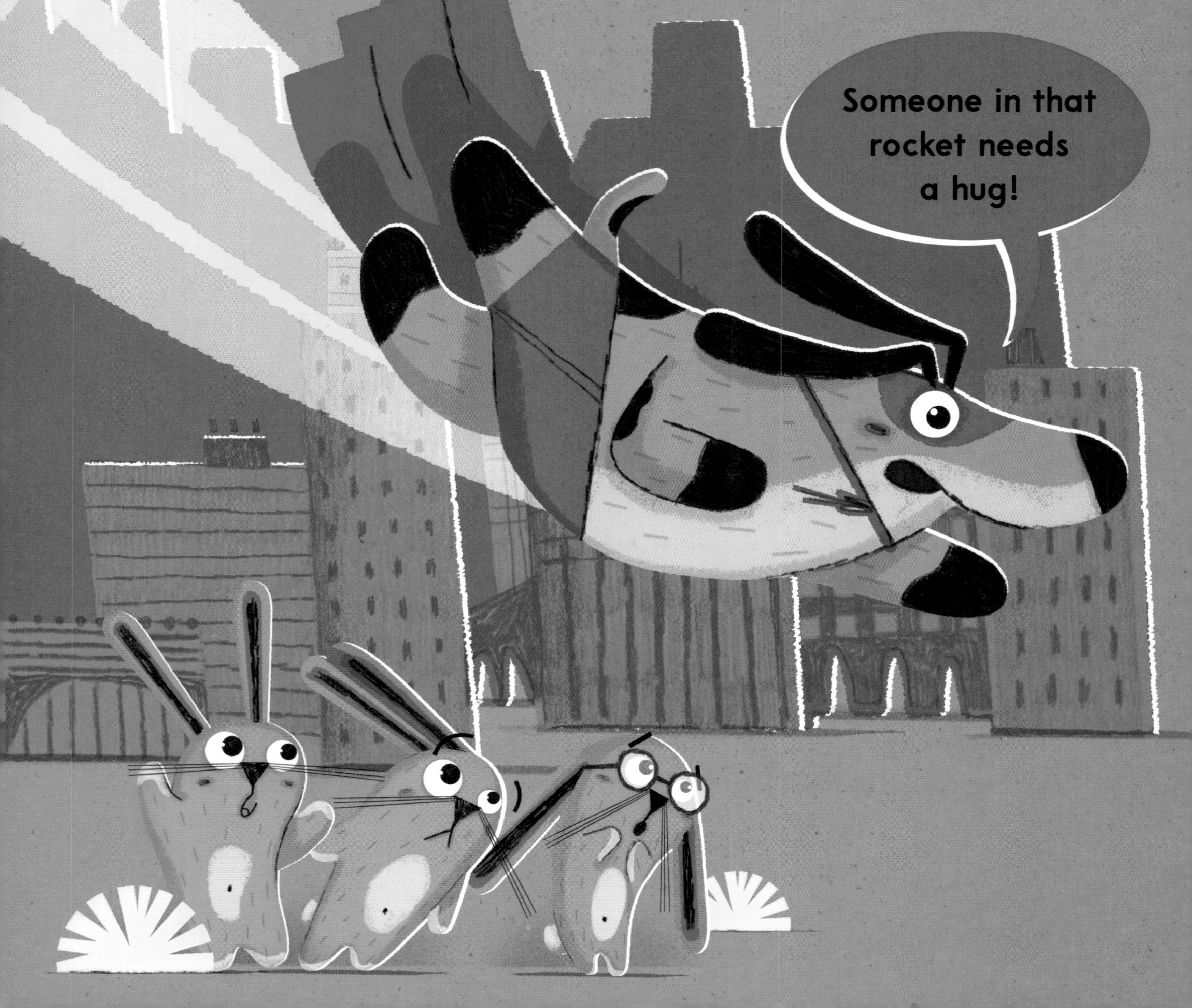

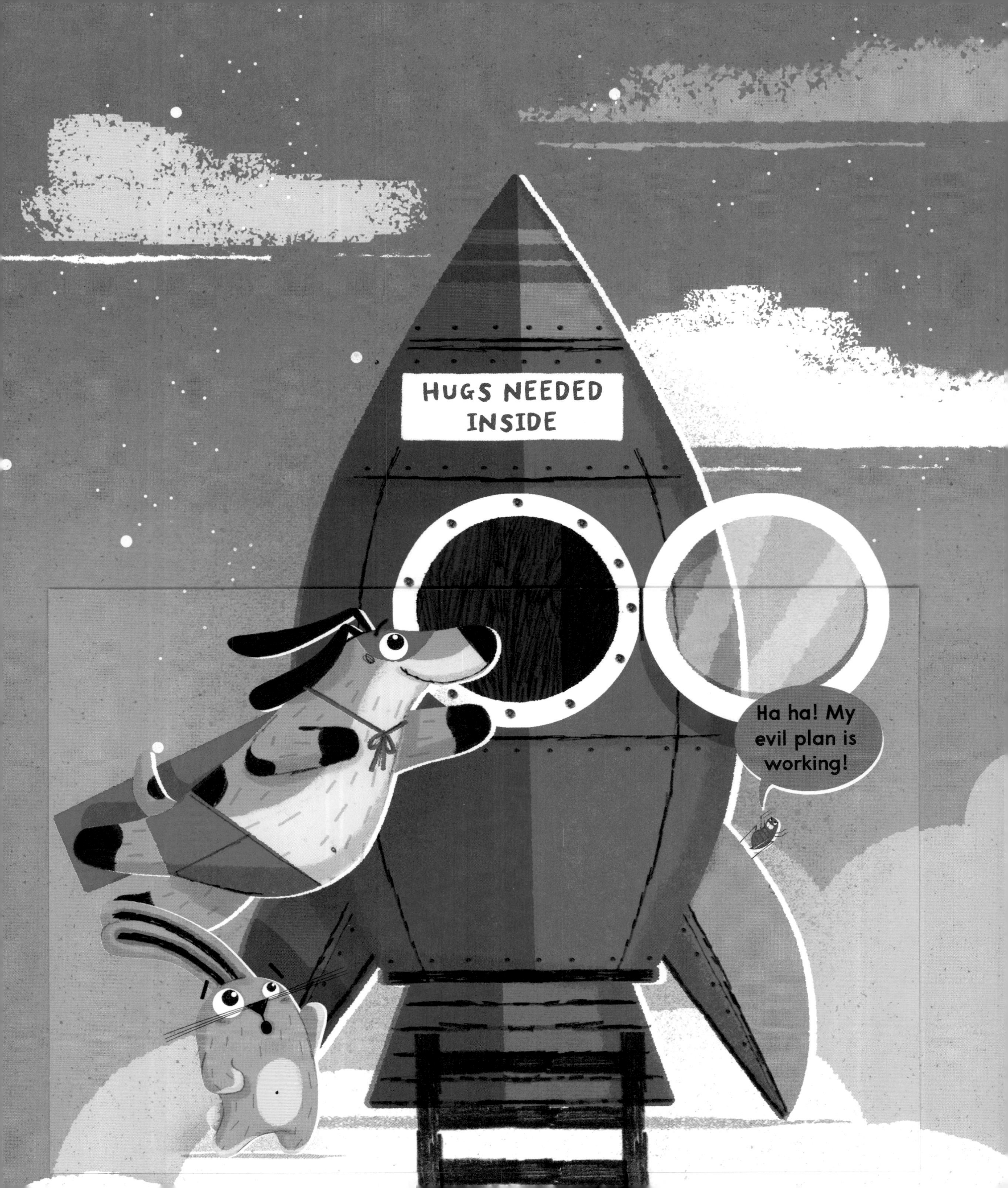
HUGS NEEDED INSIDE
Ha ha! My evil plan is working!

Poor Captain Cuddles.
His hugging days are over.
It's ever so lonely spinning
slowly through space.

Crikey, what's THAT?
Another rocket?? Yes!
They are flying to the
rescue.

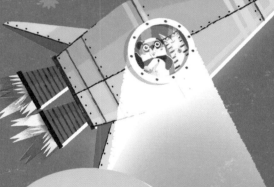

We'll save
you, Captain
Cuddles!

The world
needs your
hugs!

QUICK,

Captain Cuddles!
Stop that
dinosaur!

SQUEEZE!

Oh no, his cuddle
isn't working!

Look sharp, Cuddle Team. I see a sad flea in need of a hug.

But I'm too TEENY TINY to be cuddled. That's why I wanted to rid the world of these DEPLORABLE hugs.

NOPE. No one is too small for cuddles. Captain, you know what to do.

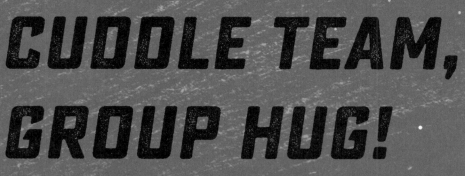

CUDDLE TEAM, GROUP HUG!